MONSTER ☠ HIGH™

DIARIES

MONSTER HIGH™ DIARIES

FRANKIE STEIN AND THE NEW GHOUL AT SCHOOL

By Nessi Monstrata

LITTLE, BROWN AND COMPANY

New York Boston

Little, Brown and Company

Hachette Book Group
1290 Avenue of the Americas, New York, NY 10104
Visit us at lb-kids.com

Little, Brown and Company is a division of Hachette Book Group, Inc.
The Little, Brown name and logo are trademarks of Hachette Book Group, Inc.

The publisher is not responsible for websites (or their content)
that are not owned by the publisher.

First Edition: November 2015

Library of Congress Cataloging-in-Publication Data

Names: Monstrata, Nessi, author.
Title: Frankie Stein and the new ghoul at school / by Nessi Monstrata.
Description: First edition. | New York ; Boston : Little, Brown and Company, 2015. |
Series: Monster High diaries | Summary: Frankie is thrilled to show Isi Dawndancer, a new student, around Monster High but when Frankie's best friends and even her pet seem to prefer the new ghoul to her, Frankie becomes lonely and confused.
Identifiers: LCCN 2015029304| ISBN 9780316300940 (pb) | ISBN 9780316300933 (ebook)
Subjects: | CYAC: Friendship—Fiction. | Pets—Fiction. | Monsters—Fiction. | High schools—Fiction. | Schools—Fiction. | Diaries—Fiction.
Classification: LCC PZ7.1.M64 Fr 2015 | DDC [Fic]—dc23 LC record available at http://lccn.loc.gov/2015029304

10 9 8 7 6 5 4 3 2

RRD-C

Printed in the United States of America

Diary Entry

Usually, my life moves at the speed of lightning...
I'm always so busy having new experiences and
tons of voltageous fun with my ghoulfriends. But
for the past week, all the students at Monster
High have been on scaremester break, and
I had no idea days could creep by so slowly. I
miss my ghoulfriends, Fearleading practice, and
everything about Monster High so much when
I'm not there!

Spending time at home with my parents over
the break has been creeperific, of course.
It's great to spend some quality time together,

getting recharged as a fam. But when school is in session, every day just buzzes with new adventure and freaky-fabulous fun. So even though I love hanging out with Mom and Dad and Watzit (my sweet little pet just <u>loves</u> that I've been home all week to cuddle with him!), I do get a little lonely here in this big house with just the four of us.

I can't wait to see my ghoulfriends again! We have <u>so much</u> to catch up on.

Frankie

CHAPTER ONE

Hey, Dad, I'm going to head over to Draculaura's castle for a bit, okay?" Frankie Stein shouted down the stairs to her father's lab. Because her dad was usually busy scaring up new inventions, she knew he might not hear her over the noise and clatter of the lab. So she stepped down a few stairs and called out, "Dad? I'll be back in a couple of hours. Okay?"

Mr. Stein peered around the corner and looked up the stairs at his daughter. He pushed his lab goggles onto his forehead and grinned. "It's alive!"

Frankie rolled her eyes good-naturedly. Every morning, her dad greeted her the same way. Mr. Stein, a mad scientist and inventor, had created Frankie in his lab. Ever since the day Frankie was first jolted to life by electricity, her dad had made it clear he was amazed by his greatest creation, and he never tired of letting Frankie know how proud he was of her. "Good morning to you too, Dad. Yeah, I'm alive—just like yesterday and the day before that. Is it okay if I go fang out at Draculaura's for a while? Clawdeen will also be there."

Mr. Stein nodded. He held a beaker full of bubbling green liquid in one hand, and there was a blob of something gooey glowing blue in the other. He held his hands up, squinting at his daughter in the bright light of the lab.

"Well, look at that! This batch matches your eyes perfectly."

Frankie traipsed the rest of the way down the stairs for a closer look at the beakers in her dad's hands. Whatever her father was holding *did* match her eyes perfectly. Frankie's left eye was a brilliant shade of green, and her right eye was bright blue. She loved that her eyes were so unique. "Whatcha makin'?" she asked, curious. She pulled her black-and-white-striped hair back, careful to keep the long strands from the glowing blob of blue in her father's gloved hand. She never knew what his potions and mixtures had the power to do, and her hair was looking scary-cute today—she didn't want anything to mess that up!

She leaned forward and sniffed—the green beaker smelled like bacon and roses. The blue blob in her dad's hand smelled like dirt. Altogether, it was not a great combo, but Frankie was sure her dad must be creating something voltageous. What her dad did in his lab all day was something of a mystery. She rarely hung out down here while he was doing his thing because she was usually at school or busy with her ghoulfriends...but she was always curious to hear more about his inventions.

"Just working on a little experiment," Mr. Stein said, distracted. "A new, secret project."

"I hope if you're making me a sister, this means she and I will have the same color eyes...?" Frankie mischievously poked at the beaker of green liquid. "*Is* that your secret project, Dad? A sister for me?" She grinned sweetly at her father. There had been a few weeks last scaremester when her dad was buried for hours on end in his lab. Curious about what he was working on, Frankie had asked her mom if perhaps her dad was hard at work on building a new sibling for her. Her mom had practically choked on her coffincino and sputtered, "Uh, no. I'm afraid not."

Now Mr. Stein shook his head and laughed. "I'll keep that in mind if and when I work on something like a sister for you, sweetheart. But at the moment, a sibling is certainly *not* what I'm working on. Do you want to spend the day helping me out in the lab and I can show you around a little?" He wiggled his thick eyebrows and gently plopped the blue blob into a beaker. As if on cue, the blob wiggled and began to rise up in the tube. "We can have some fun."

Frankie was torn. She really did want to help her dad—spending the day in the lab with him sounded like a creeperific time, and Frankie loved new experiences. But she had been waiting to see her ghoulfriends for what felt like forever, and she knew her ghouls were as eager to see her as she was to see them. Frankie didn't want to disappoint them.

"Another day?" she asked.

"You're on." Her dad nodded and turned away, already lost in his own world. He nearly tripped and fell as he walked away, as he was too busy muttering strange number patterns and words to himself to pay attention to his own two feet. Frankie watched as the blob of blue goo rose up out of the beaker in her father's hand and landed on the floor with a plop! It glowed, pulsed, and then slithered away, Mr. Stein chasing after it.

Frankie giggled. "Have some freaky fun with your creations in the lab today. I'll be home in time for dinner! Maybe we can order a cheese screechza for dinner?"

"Yes. *Yes*...!" Mr. Stein said distractedly, from deep in the lab.

"Yay!" Frankie looked around the corner and smiled at him as he scooped up the blob.

"Wait—what? Screechza?" he said, shaking his head to clear it.

But Frankie was already gone. She waved, then ran back up the stairs and out the front door.

Diary Entry

Whenever I'm not at school, I crave the energy of Monster High—it makes me feel so alive, like right after I've had a full charge! That's why I'm always asking Dad about a new sibling...because someday, I really do think it would be <u>VOLTAGEOUS</u> to have a full house.

When Clawdeen talks about her school breaks, she growls about how her house feels jam-packed and filled with craziness because she has so many family members. Even though I know they make her crazy sometimes, I also know how much she loves having a full den. Someone is always up for watching a boo-vie or playing a game or going for a run or whatever. At our house, it's just my dad's lab full of freaky-fab projects, one adorable pet, and the three of us Steins.

Sometimes I wonder what it would be like if I had a pack too. I'll have to ask Clawdeen if I can borrow a few of her sibs sometime to see what it would be like to be surrounded the way she usually is! I'm sure she wouldn't mind a little break from all that action. ☺

Frankie

CHAPTER TWO

When she got to Draculaura's house a short while later, Frankie lifted the huge knocker on the castle's front door and let it crash down with a resounding thud. A moment later, Draculaura flung the door open and exclaimed, "I thought you would never get here!" Frankie's always-cheerful ghoulfriend gave her a hug. She broke into a huge smile, revealing two adorable vampire fangs, and her cheeks flushed a deeper pink color as she squeezed Frankie tight. "Come in, come in. I can't wait to show you something. I bought you a little present on my trip this week, and I'm so excited for you to see it!"

Frankie smiled happily. Draculaura loved helping Frankie shop for clothes—and Frankie loved having her help. Frankie's beast ghoulfriends, Draculaura and Clawdeen Wolf, had spooktacular style, and they were always happy to share their fashion wisdom with Frankie by helping her put together creepy-cool outfits. Frankie had no doubt that Draculaura's present was a piece of clothing.

Draculaura chatted excitedly about her latest trip as she led Frankie through the winding halls of the castle. Frankie was always amazed at the beauty of Draculaura's home. When Draculaura and her father had left Transylvania many years earlier, Dracula had all the pieces of their castle shipped over to the Boo World and reassembled. Their castle looks just like the one they'd had in

Transylvania, which Draculaura said helped to make the Boo World feel more like home when they had first arrived. Of course, now Draculaura loved the Boo World and was totally thrilled to be attending Monster High.

Frankie followed her friend to her bedroom, which was decorated in wall-to-wall pink, Draculaura's favorite color. Clawdeen was waiting for them there, sprawled out on Draculaura's floor. The contents of Draculaura's closet were thrown across every surface—it was clear that Clawdeen and Draculaura had been preparing outfits for the coming week of school while they waited for Frankie to arrive.

"Check out the fierce skirt Draculaura got for you, Frankie!" Clawdeen exclaimed as she leaped nimbly up off Draculaura's floor and rushed over to greet Frankie with a kiss on the cheek. The bold and beautiful werewolf held up a black-and-white-striped skirt with purple lace stitching. "This is going to look clawesome on you!"

Draculaura bounced up and down in excitement. "Isn't it fangtastic? Try it on, Frankie! It will look totes adorable with the shirt you're wearing right now."

Frankie stepped into a corner to change. Meanwhile, Clawdeen pawed through Draculaura's jewelry stash and found a few things she wanted to borrow for their first week back at school. "You have no idea how great it is to be with you ghouls again," Clawdeen said, letting out a sigh that sounded more like a growl. "I am so ready for the scaremester break to be over."

"Same here," Frankie said.

"Did I miss anything fun while I was gone?" Draculaura asked.

"Actually, I have news!" Clawdeen said excitedly. "Clawd met up with some of the other guys to play Casketball yesterday, and Deuce said that he heard from Cleo that there are a few new Monster Exchange students coming to Monster High after the break."

"New ghouls?" Frankie wondered.

"I think so," Clawdeen said. "Apparently Headmistress Bloodgood is looking for students who might be willing to show them around during their first week at Monster High. You know, Monster Exchange buddies."

Frankie felt a bolt of excitement rush through her body. "I would love to do something like that! I remember exactly what it was like to be the new ghoul at school, and it would be voltageous to make sure the new students feel welcome right away!" Frankie's mind was going a mile a minute as she thought about how much she wanted to be a Monster Exchange buddy to one of the new ghouls. "It's hard to start at a new school when you don't know anyone! Where do I sign up?"

"You'd be such a great Monster Exchange buddy," Draculaura agreed. "You know better than anyone that a new student needs to feel welcome during their first week. You should definitely tell the headmistress you want to do it, Frankie."

Frankie's entire body was buzzing with excitement. She tried to rein in her enthusiasm. Sometimes, when she got *too* excited about things, she would spark—and that had caused a few problems in the past. She tried taking a deep breath to calm herself down. "I'm going to drop by the headmistress's office first thing tomorrow morning," Frankie proclaimed happily. Then she stepped into her new skirt and pranced into the center of the room to model it for her ghoulfriends. "What do you think?"

Draculaura cheered. "I knew it would look fangulous on you. Oh, I'm so glad I bought it.

You have to wear it on the first day back after break, okay?"

"That will be the perfect outfit to wear for your fall project presentation," Clawdeen added. "Scary-cute, smart, *and* sophisticated!"

When she heard the words *fall project presentation*, Frankie's excitement fizzled. "Ugh. Our fall project..."

"You did finish your project...right?" Clawdeen asked slowly.

"Um," Frankie mumbled. "I haven't exactly started. I haven't had my spark of inspiration yet, so I'm totally stuck!" Everyone at Monster High had been asked to do an independent study project over break. They were supposed to do a project and put together a presentation that would give their classmates a behind-the-scenes look at what kinds of things they liked to do in their time away from school.

They had been given total freedom with the project. Monster High students were allowed to do an art project, write a story, complete a research project about a place they had visited, build or sew something...anything. The great thing about this project was that they were allowed to do anything that got their sparks flying.

Clawdeen's eyes widened. "We're supposed to present our projects in class on Monday! I stitched up one of the pieces in the clothing line I've been designing, to show everyone my freaky fashion skills."

"That's a great idea, Clawdeen," Frankie said. Usually, Frankie was the kind of ghoul who finished her schoolwork right away—but with this fall project presentation, she was stuck. "I can't come up with anything to do for the presentation."

"Don't worry about it," Draculaura said, trying to be as encouraging as possible. "There are still four days left before school is back in session. You still have time to come up with something totes amazing for your project."

Frankie took another deep breath, her good mood crashing to the castle floor. She couldn't believe there were only four days left to start and finish her fall scaremester project! What if she couldn't come up with anything?

When Frankie had first heard about the assignment, she decided that she wanted to do something that gave her classmates some insight into what made her special and different from every other monster. If there was one thing Frankie was sure of, it was that freaky flaws were meant to be celebrated. But what kind of project could she do that celebrated what made her special?

Remembering how excited she had been about the project when they first heard about it, Frankie couldn't believe she hadn't come up with anything yet. Usually, school projects really sparked her excitement. She tried not to worry herself too much. Because Draculaura was right—she still had four days to develop something fearsome. As far as she was concerned, only one question needed to be answered....

Frankie grinned at her ghoulfriends. "So, do either of you have any idea what I should do for my project?"

Diary Entry

My ghoulfriends helped me come up with the most voltageous idea for my fall project! Since Dad is the greatest inventor of <u>all time</u> (I may be a little biased!), we realized he and I could work on building something together in his lab. What better way to share what makes me special with everyone at Monster High than to create something in the very lab where I was created?

Dad invited me to join him in the lab yesterday, so I just know he'll say yes. And the best part of this idea is, I can bring my creation to school for the presentation. An actual creation that I've built in the lab will be so creepy-cool to show everyone!

The one problem I have is time. With only three days left until the end of the scaremester break, I have to get to work right away! I know it took years for Dad to bring me to life, so I hope it's possible to build something cool in just a few days...!

Maybe while I'm working on building my invention, Dad could get to work creating a new sibling for me.... It can't hurt to keep asking, right?

I would have gotten started on my project already, but I had something else I had to do this morning—something just as exciting! I went to see Headmistress Bloodgood to tell her I'd like to be one of the Monster Exchange program buddies. She said that she was really happy I was interested and that she would e-mail me this weekend to let me know if I'm in. Fingers crossed!

Frankie

CHAPTER THREE

As soon as Frankie returned home from her visit to the headmistress's office the next morning, she hustled to her dad's lab. Watzit trailed behind her, yapping at her legs, begging for a game of fetch. Frankie had a feeling her pet could sense that the scaremester break was almost over, and he was trying to spend as much time with her as possible. She loved having so much time to play with him and knew she would miss their special cuddle time when she was back at school all day the next week.

"It's alive!" Mr. Stein bellowed when he saw his daughter round the corner into his part of the lab. A portion of the laboratory had been carved out to use as Frankie's bedroom when she was brought to life, and it was Frankie's very favorite place to fang out—but the other side of the lab remained Mr. Stein's lair.

Frankie laughed. "Yes, Dad, I'm alive," she agreed. "Just like yesterday and the day before and the day before that and…" She glanced around the lab, curious about which of the mysterious machines and tools they would be using to build her creation.

"And how are you this morning, my greatest creation?" Frankie's dad put down a beaker filled with yellow liquid and turned off a machine that was buzzing loudly nearby. Frankie loved that her dad was always willing to set everything else aside for a chat with her. She knew he was very busy with his work, but he always had time for her. And she felt a little jolt of happiness each and every time her dad referred to her as his greatest creation.

"I'm sparktacular actually," Frankie said, beaming. "If you have a couple of minutes, I need to talk to you about something important."

"Excellent," Mr. Stein said. "Let's head up to the kitchen and discuss it over a coffincino. Your mom is always telling me I should step out of the lab for a few minutes each day to get some fresh air. Sound good?"

"Yes. And I agree with Mom. You spend so much time down here. I could help you redecorate the space a little bit—add a few personal touches, so it's not so... 'lab-ish'?"

"What's wrong with 'lab-ish'?" Mr. Stein asked.

Frankie took another look around. The space was filled with rusty machines and colorful beakers of liquid and creations that were half-assembled. In its own way, the lab was pretty creeperific. It was certainly decorated in a different style than Draculaura's castle or Cleo de Nile's elegant palace, but Frankie liked it and realized she felt comfortable here. Maybe lab chic was her thing?

Back upstairs, Frankie got herself a snack and settled in at the table across from her dad. Frankie's mom looked up from her book and smiled. "Good morning, sweetheart. Anything special planned for today?"

Frankie briefly told her parents how she was hoping to be chosen as one of the Monster Exchange program buddies. "I would love to show one of the new ghouls around school!"

"Well," said her mom, "it sounds like a really nice way to help out. I'm glad you're stepping up to be a part of it."

Frankie's dad took a sip of his coffincino and coughed. "Hot! Ow, that's hot! I really ought to build a coffincino machine that brews coffee at just the right temperature. It comes out of our machine too hot." He ripped a scrap of paper off the bottom of Frankie's mom's newspaper and jotted a note to himself.

"Perhaps," Mrs. Stein suggested, giving him a sideways look, "if you just took a moment to sit and relax while your coffee cooled, you wouldn't always burn yourself. You are allowed to slow down and relax every now and again...."

Mr. Stein grinned sheepishly. "I could do that too. But there's just so much to do, and so little time!" He turned to Frankie. "You said you wanted to talk about something. Now, what's on your mind?"

"I have such a voltageous idea I can hardly stand it!" She pushed aside her plate and continued.

"I'd like to work with you to build something of my very own in the lab!" The smile that crept onto her dad's face made Frankie's heart swell with happiness. "We were assigned a project over the scaremester break. It's an independent study project of our choice—and I want to do something that will show the other students at Monster High who I am and what it's like to be in my family. I think the best way to show everyone a little something about who *we* are would be to build something in the lab! With you, Dad! We get to present our project on Monday, the day we get back from break."

Frankie's dad was nodding enthusiastically as he took in everything his daughter had said, but her mom looked less excited. Frankie's mom spoke first. "This project is due on Monday? And we're just hearing about it...now? That's three days away!"

Frankie shrugged. "Um, yes?"

"Frankie, this is so last-minute!" her mother scolded. "You're usually much better about staying on top of your homework."

"I know," Frankie said with a sigh. "It took me a long time to come up with the perfect idea. But it can be done! Right, Dad?"

Mr. Stein gulped down the last of his still-scalding coffincino. He cringed, his face turning bright red from the burning coffee. "So hot!" he cried, then leaped to his feet. "But a few coffee burns are certainly worth it, in the name of science and inventions. Of course this can be done, Frankie! No challenge is too great for a great inventor. But if we're going to make something truly spooktacular, we need to get started right away."

"That's what I was hoping you'd say," Frankie cheered.

Frankie's mom couldn't help but smile at her husband's and daughter's enthusiasm. "All right, it sounds like you two had better get to work!" she said. "But, Frankie, keep in mind that leaving things until the last minute is never a good idea. Please try harder to stay on top of your assignments and responsibilities in the future...."

Frankie met her mom's eyes and nodded solemnly. "I promise, Mom."

"Okay, then get to work!" her mom replied, giving her a quick hug.

Feeling so excited that her stitches could burst, Frankie made her way down to the lab after her father. "So, here's what I was thinking," she began. "What if I build myself a new pet? I feel so bad about leaving Watzit home alone while I'm at school all day, and it could be fun for us to create a new little critter for him to play with. What do you think?"

"Hmmm," Mr. Stein said. "A new pet, eh?"

"Or we could try to make me a sister?" she said with a sly smile. "Or a brother. A little brother could be just as interesting as a sister...."

"Frankie," Mr. Stein said in a warning tone. "You know that's out of the question at the moment. My work to build you took years, and we only have three days, so we need to be reasonable—"

Frankie nodded, giggling. "I know, I know. I just like to remind you, every now and again, that it *would* be nice to have a sister or brother sometime."

Mr. Stein shook his head. "Enough discussion of siblings for now. Don't you think we already make a nice little family of three? You're certainly more amazing than your mother and I ever could have hoped for."

Frankie laughed. "Just consider it—but for now, do you think we really could make another pet? Watzit would be so excited!" At her feet, Watzit sat and wagged his tail happily. "See? He loves the idea of me building him a new fiend!"

"I suppose a new pet is a possibility," Mr. Stein replied. "Have you drawn up any plans? Of course, that's the first step to every great invention: a plan!"

"As a matter of fact, I have," Frankie said proudly. She had been watching her father's work closely enough from afar that she already knew how important it was to plan before just jumping into things. She grabbed the designs she had sketched the night before and that morning and set them on the lab bench. "Ta-da!"

Mr. Stein leaned in close. Frankie waited nervously for him to say something. Eventually, he murmured, "Ah yes...I see...I like what you've done here. Yes, yes, this is brilliant."

"Really?" Frankie squealed. She had drawn up designs for a tiny critter, just about the same size as

Watzit. Her body would be stitched together using spare parts that were lying around the lab—there were plenty to choose from! Frankie had seen some creeperific plaid fabric in Clawdeen's bedroom and hoped she might be able to persuade her friend to sew her new pet and Watzit matching sweaters. They would be so scary-cute! She was thrilled to hear that her dad was impressed.

"Before we begin," Mr. Stein said, bustling around the lab, "I need to go through some important rules for the lab. Safety is essential, of course—and I want you to feel totally comfortable while you're working in here. When an inventor feels relaxed and confident in the lab, that's when the best ideas emerge."

For the next hour, Mr. Stein walked Frankie all around the lab, showing her how everything worked. He introduced her to machines whose names she couldn't pronounce, and let her touch substances that were so powerful that—if mixed incorrectly—could destroy Monster High.

Frankie was overwhelmed by everything and quickly realized that what her father did for a living was way more complicated than she had realized. But as he spoke, she took careful notes and felt like she was really able to follow along. She was totally at home in the lab—just like her dad—and couldn't wait to get started!

She was so eager, in fact, that when her dad stepped around to the back of a machine to fix a loose wire and it took longer than a few moments, Frankie decided to start working on her project on her own. She grabbed the welder her dad had showed her how to use and fused two pieces of sheet metal together into something that would work perfectly as the back and shoulders of her new pet. Then she found four tubes that would work as legs and began sawing at them to make them equal lengths. She didn't want any rough edges, so Frankie carefully buffed them all until they were smooth. She could feel the energy coursing through her body—the lab made her feel every bit as alive as a full electrical charge. No wonder her dad loved inventing so much!

Mr. Stein stood proudly to the side and watched as his daughter rushed around the lab, pushing buttons and letting sparks fly. Her hair stood on end, and her skin glowed an even brighter green than usual. Though Frankie still had a lot to learn, her dad chose to stay out of her way so she could learn through trial and error. After all, he knew his greatest inventions had come after many false starts.

Frankie flipped a switch on one of the machines and felt a jolt. *Zap!* She was blasted backward. She crashed into the lab table behind her, sending a beaker filled with lime-green goo spilling onto the table. The thick liquid oozed over the table's black surface, leaving a bright green trail in its wake. Several drops of the goo splattered onto the floor, where they exploded with a pop!

Now Mr. Stein jumped into action. He grabbed a cloth and tossed it onto the spill—but he wasn't quite fast enough. Some of the green goo had oozed under a pile of spare parts that were waiting to be used for something later. Coated in the thick green liquid, the spare parts began to zap and fizz like fireworks. Frankie and her dad dived for cover under a lab bench.

Frankie's eyes were wide. She felt awful! This was her first time working in the lab, and she had scared up a disaster. "I'm so sorry," she said quickly. "I didn't mean for this to happen! I can't believe I made such a big mistake...."

But to her relief, Mr. Stein laughed. "Frankie, this is all part of being an inventor—sometimes, things go according to plan; other times, they do not. It's all part of the process!"

Another pop rocked the room, and the buzzing sounds intensified. Mr. Stein shrugged his shoulders and said, "Luckily, this is all easily fixed. No worries, dear." He patted Frankie on the cheek. "Your next task is to clean up and begin again. After all, nothing great was ever created without a few problems along the way."

Diary Entry

I'm having the <u>beast time</u> working with my dad in the lab! We spent all afternoon yesterday working on the moving parts for my new pet. I decided to call this little critter Zappit...because it seems like every time I make a mistake, one of Dad's machines zaps me! There's been a lot of zapping going on! ☺

  We only have today and tomorrow left to finish up, and then it will be time for my creeperific reveal. I'm so happy my ghoulfriends and I came up with this idea for my fall project. Of course, I had no idea just how hard it would be to bring a little creature to life. I'm amazed at everything my dad has been able to accomplish in his lab over the past few years. No wonder it seems like he's always working—inventions take a monstrous amount of time!

I'm building Zappit out of some mint-green spare parts I found around the lab that match my skin color perfectly. I'm combining them with a few parts Dad had left over from when he created Watzit. So Zappit's coloring will be a voltageous combo of me and Watzit! And, of course, just like the two of us, she'll have one blue eye and one green eye.

This morning, when we tried to power up Zappit, she let out the most <u>adorable</u> little growl, and when she moved, it almost seemed as if she were dancing. Then she short-circuited, and I had to turn her off for further adjustments—but as Dad pointed out, these are all important hiccups that need to be overcome for a successful invention!

Zappit still has a few glitches, but I think she should be done in time for me to take her into school on Monday for my presentation. My little creation and I are going to knock everyone dead during my presentation!

Frankie

CHAPTER FOUR

Frankie and her dad had been working in the lab almost nonstop for over a day. Frankie hadn't even stopped to sleep, but she did hook herself up for a full charge late in the night after they'd been working for many hours. By Saturday afternoon, Mrs. Stein forced Frankie to reemerge from the basement to have some lunch. Reluctantly, she climbed up the steps feeling both weary and excited.

"Have you heard from Headmistress Bloodgood about the Monster Exchange buddy program yet?" her mom asked as Frankie sat down for lunch. As soon as she started digging in to the grilled cheese her mom had made for her, she realized just how hungry she was!

"Not yet—but I haven't even had time to check in with her," Frankie admitted between bites. She'd been so wrapped up in her lab work that she had almost forgotten about her conversation with the headmistress. She scarfed down the rest of her sandwich, plus an apple and a chocolate chip cookie, then logged on to check her e-mail. Yes! There it was. "Mom, I'm in!" She scanned the e-mail, learning that she was to report to the headmistress's office first thing Monday to meet her new buddy.

Mrs. Stein hustled over and read the e-mail over Frankie's shoulder. "Isi Dawndancer? What an interesting name."

Frankie buzzed with excitement. "She sounds voltageous!"

Mrs. Stein laughed. "You don't know anything about her."

"But if she wants to come to Monster High, she must be voltageous, right? I can't wait to introduce her to everyone and show her around. Wouldn't it be exciting if she were interested in joining the Fearleading squad? Of course, if she's not a great dancer, it's no big deal—I'll teach her everything she needs to know. And she can sit with us at lunch, and maybe we can take her shopping this weekend for some spooktacular new clothes—"

"Don't get ahead of yourself," Mrs. Stein warned. "You're just like your dad, Frankie. You let your excitement about new things energize you so much you have a hard time winding down." She smiled at her daughter. "I'm so happy you've volunteered to be a part of this, though.

It's great to see you fitting in so well at Monster High."

Frankie smiled back. She really was having a creeperific time at Monster High. She loved her classes, and she adored her ghoulfriends. Draculaura and Clawdeen had made her feel like part of the group from her very first day—freaky flaws and everything—and now she would have the opportunity to pay it forward. She was sure Isi Dawndancer would become one of her closest ghoulfriends too in no time.

Watzit pawed at Frankie's leg, and she bent down to give him a scratch. "Is it time to get back to the lab, little one?" she cooed. "I bet you're ready for me to finish Zappit so you two can play, huh? Are you?" Of course, Watzit didn't answer. But Frankie was pretty sure he was as excited about her invention as she was. Who didn't love new fiends?

She grabbed a second cookie off the counter and dashed out of the kitchen. "Heading back to the lab, Mom. See you for dinner. Maybe."

"Don't drain your batteries too much," her mom called after her. "You need to save some of your energy for school on Monday!"

"I won't," Frankie hollered back. She raced down to the lab, ready to get back to work. When she got downstairs, she found her dad was busy working on one of his own projects on the far side of the lab. So Frankie picked up just where she'd left off with Zappit, and she and her dad worked side by side for the next few hours. Every so often, Mr. Stein would lean over and make a suggestion when it was clear Frankie was stuck. But for the most part, Frankie worked independently. She had gone from stranger to expert in the lab! She felt like she was made to do this sort of work, and in a way, she was!

After she had been working for a while, Frankie set up a little bed for Watzit on the floor so he would feel like he was in on the action too. As she worked, Frankie snapped pictures of the progress she was making. She wanted to be able to show her classmates what it took to build her creation when she presented it to the class on Monday. No one would believe how much work it took to build a little critter!

Frankie swelled with pride when—finally— hours after her family's usual dinner time, she was able to announce, "It's alive!" The little critter Frankie had created stretched, yawned, and released a small growl. Watzit jumped out of his bed and stared at the little beast, yapping madly as the new creature danced and wiggled around in circles atop the lab table. Frankie leaned down and whispered, "Shhhh, it's okay, Watzit. This is your new friend! I think you two are going to be beast fiends forever, aren't you? Aren't you? I made her just for you!"

Zappit growled at Watzit, then Watzit hid behind Frankie's legs. Frankie laughed, picked up her new pet, and snuggled her close against her chest. Zappit squirmed, and Frankie let her down to shimmy across the tabletop again. Frankie couldn't believe she had done it—her very first invention. It was *alive*!

Mr. Stein clapped and congratulated her. "A job well done! You should be very proud. You're a natural in the lab."

"Do you think so?" Frankie asked, but she knew the answer. She *was* a natural in the lab. She should have joined her father ages ago! She would have to thank her teachers for assigning the fall project—without it, she might never have realized what a great inventor she was! She couldn't wait to figure out what she might create next. Suddenly, the exhaustion of the last few days caught up to her. Frankie yawned, then collapsed on one of the chairs nearby.

"You're fried," her dad said.

Frankie yawned again. "You're right. I'm totally drained." She began to clean up her mess, but her dad held out his hand to stop her.

"I'll clean up," he said. "You should get some rest. Take tomorrow to relax, download your pictures, and put together your presentation for school on Monday."

"Thanks, Dad." Frankie tucked a squirming Zappit under her arm and began to head toward her room with Watzit close at her heels.

"Frankie," her dad said, chasing after her. "Zappit needs to spend a few hours in the lab before you can play with her. She needs a full charge to work properly. Let her rest here overnight, and the two of you can get to know each other in the morning."

"Really?" Frankie sighed. "But I wanted to bring her into my room tonight so she and Watzit could play!"

Her dad smiled. "I know it's tempting to play with your new inventions right away. But it's important to take your time. Just like you, she'll need a full charge to be fully energized. If you let her charge up overnight, her battery will last several days before she needs a jolt of power again. Trust me. You can spend all day tomorrow bonding before school starts."

Diary Entry

Oh. My. Ghoul! Zappit is missing! After such a long day in the lab yesterday, Mom let me sleep late this morning so I could be totally recharged for school. I woke up to the sound of Watzit's yapping. He was whining at the foot of my bed and tugging at my covers, so I got up and followed him. He led me to Zappit's charging station, and that's when I saw that she was gone!

The only thing Dad and I can figure out is that my new creation must have wandered off sometime in the night. This is a voltageous fail! I never should have taken my eyes off her. Watzit has spent the whole morning right by my side, and I'm so glad—there's no way I'm going to let my pet out of my sight. I've already lost one of my dear pets; I can't possibly risk losing another.

I texted my ghoulfriends, and they all offered to spend the day helping me look for Zappit. Watzit is going to come along in case he can help track her scent. Dad's taking the day off from working in the lab so he and Mom can search too.

On top of being <u>so worried</u> about poor Zappit, I'm also worried about what will happen when I turn up at school tomorrow without having a finished assignment. Showing off Zappit was the beast part of my whole presentation—without her, it won't be nearly as special. What's a ghoul to do?

Frankie

CHAPTER FIVE

On Monday morning, Frankie woke up feeling less than sparktacular. Though she and her ghoulfriends had searched for Zappit all day on Sunday—the last day of their scaremester break—her sweet little pet was nowhere to be found. She and her parents and ghoulfriends had looked everywhere, but it was as though the little beast had simply disappeared. They had run out of ideas about where to search, and Frankie was sick with worry. She spent Sunday night curled up with Watzit, who happily gave her the extra helping of cuddles she needed.

As Frankie got ready for her first day back at school, the only thing keeping her from short-circuiting in a pool of tears was the fact that she would get to meet her new Monster Exchange buddy that morning. Even though she had lost her pet and was probably about to fail her assignment, at least she got to make a new ghoulfriend and be a part of making someone else's day go well. That was enough to energize her at least a little bit.

Frankie smiled as she remembered the advice Draculaura had given her the previous day. "You have to believe in your bolts that Zappit will be okay," Draculaura had told her. "And until you find her, you should try to think about something else—something fangtastic, like meeting Isi Dawndancer and giving her a totes amazing welcome to Monster High!" Frankie knew

Draculaura was right—she had to focus on helping Isi Dawndancer have a great first day at Monster High.

As she got dressed, Frankie thought about how grateful she was that Draculaura had bought her the new skirt. Having a creepy-cool outfit ready meant she didn't have to waste any extra time on choosing something to wear, and she was able to spend a few minutes before school searching and putting up MISSING posters. But still, she had no idea where else she could look to find Zappit. She just couldn't imagine where the little creature might have gone.

Frankie arrived at the headmistress's office about twenty minutes before school began, eager to meet Isi Dawndancer. When she got there, a ghoul came dancing over to her and asked, "Any chance you're Frankie Stein?"

Frankie looked at her, surprised. "I am." The ghoul seemed to be bursting with energy, and her outfit was to die for—a loose, flowy turquoise minidress and killer fringed boots. As she spun and danced in the hall beside Frankie, her dress fanned out around her.

The ghoul grinned and said, "I'm Isi Dawndancer, one of the new Monster Exchange students starting at Monster High today. I'm here on an exchange from Boo Hexico, and I just heard you're going to be my Monster Exchange buddy. I'm so excited to be here!" Isi's eyes sparkled in the lights of the hall as she spun and danced to a silent beat.

"Oh!" Frankie exclaimed. "If you're Isi, then yes! I was chosen to be your Monster Exchange buddy. Maybe you already know this, but that means I will show you around to your classes and introduce you to some of the other students. I'm going to do everything I can to help you feel at home here at Monster High!" Frankie beamed at Isi. They were going to be fast ghoulfriends— Frankie could tell already!

Isi nodded enthusiastically. "The headmistress told me all about you. I was a little nervous about this Monster Exchange, but I just have a feeling I'm meant to be here at Monster High with all of you."

Frankie realized that her new ghoulfriend had barely stood still since they had met. "I'm getting the impression you really like to dance, huh?" Frankie said. She couldn't help but feel energized around Isi.

"I *love* to dance!" Isi exclaimed. Then she patted her skirt flat and stood still. She looked a little embarrassed. "Dancing is sort of my thing. Sometimes, I just can't help myself, and I break out into spontaneous dance. I feel the movement washing over me and I go with it." She shrugged. "Totally freaky, right?"

"Freaky-*fab* for sure," Frankie replied, laughing. "If dancing's your thing, then go for it!" At Monster High, everyone had something that set them apart...something that made them totally unique and different from all the other students. That's what made it such a special place to go to school—everyone's freaky flaws were recognized and, better yet, appreciated and celebrated. It was one of the things Frankie loved most about Monster High.

As she watched Isi twirl gracefully around her, Frankie thought about the Fearleading squad and said, "My ghoulfriend Cleo de Nile is going to love meeting you!"

Just then, Frankie noticed two other unfamiliar ghouls standing nearby. The headmistress stepped out of her office and said, "Ah, Frankie. I see you've already met your Monster Exchange buddy, Isi Dawndancer. Isi is the daughter of a deer spirit! I hope you're getting to know each other. This is Batsy Claro and Kjersti Trollsønn. They're the two other students who will be joining us this scaremester."

Kjersti Trollsønn, the daughter of a troll, looked up from her handheld video game and briefly made eye contact with Frankie. Frankie said a quick hello and complimented the new ghoul on her scary-cute retro-looking skirt. Kjersti reminded Frankie a bit of her ghoulfriend Ghoulia Yelps. Ghoulia always had her nose in a book or game, just like Kjersti did at the moment.

"Kjersti is from Goreway," Headmistress Bloodgood continued. "Her parents are off on an expedition, so she'll be spending the scaremester with us at Monster High." The headmistress looked up and smiled as Ghoulia slowly slumped toward them in the hall. "Ah, here's your Monster Exchange buddy now, Kjersti. Ghoulia, I believe you and Kjersti have met already and will continue to get along very well." Frankie smiled to herself at the perfect match as the headmistress added, "Thank you for agreeing to keep Kjersti company in her first week at Monster High, Ghoulia."

Ghoulia lifted her nose out of her book, pushed her red cat's-eye glasses up on her nose, and blinked. Ghoulia and Kjersti nodded hello to each other, then quietly made their way down the hall side by side, each lost in her own world.

Batsy Claro, the daughter of a white vampire bat was, on the other hand, quite chatty. "Hi," she said to Frankie. "I'm visiting from Costa Shrieka. Have you ever been to the jungle?"

"No," Frankie said, her eyes wide. "I would love to see it sometime, though!" Frankie took in Batsy's voltageous outfit—it was bright and cheerful, all vibrant pinks and greens, like a vase of fresh-cut flowers.

When Frankie complimented Batsy's outfit and told her what it reminded her of, Batsy looked alarmed. "Oh! One should *never* cut flowers from the soil simply to put them in a vase, where their only purpose would be to wilt and die. Flora is meant to be worshipped in its natural habitat."

"I guess I never thought about it that way," Frankie said with a small shrug. She felt a little awkward until Batsy smiled at her, and then Frankie realized that Batsy hadn't been scolding her—just sharing her opinion. Before the ghouls could talk more, Headmistress Bloodgood continued her introduction. "Batsy and I met when she took me and some of the other Monster High teachers on a tour around the jungle last summer," she explained to Frankie. "I learned quite a lot about the exotic animals and the beauty of the Costa Shriekan jungle. Batsy has a true appreciation for the natural world around her. She's a real outdoor lover."

"Maybe sometime you could show me around Costa Shrieka?" Frankie asked. "I'd love to see the jungle and learn more about it."

Batsy nodded enthusiastically, and her grin widened. "It would be an honor."

The headmistress nodded and then gestured down the hallway. "Ah, and here comes Venus

McFlytrap. Batsy, I think Venus will make an excellent Monster Exchange buddy for you. Let me introduce you to each other." Batsy waved good-bye, and she and the headmistress walked away, leaving Frankie and Isi alone again.

Frankie realized that the headmistress had worked really hard to pair up the new ghouls with buddies who would be a perfect fit—so that meant she also thought Frankie and Isi would make a perfect pair of ghoulfriends! Frankie felt even more sure that they were destined to be beasties. She wondered briefly how Isi would fit in with Clawdeen and Draculaura. Would they feel an instant connection to the new ghoul too? She was sure they could all work it out.

"So, have you met anyone else at Monster High yet?" Frankie asked Isi as they set off in search of Isi's locker.

"Just one ghoul," Isi said, her face lighting up. "Her name is Twyla. We met for a fleeting moment under the light of a golden moon, back home before I left—Twyla is part of the reason I'm here actually."

Frankie knew Twyla too. She was a very sweet ghoul who was also a bit shy. "Well, we'll have to find Twyla later so you two can get caught up."

As Frankie helped Isi unload her things into her locker, Isi said, "I'm so glad to have you helping me out this week. It was really hard for me to leave my family and all the animals that surround our home. The birds of the air and the beasts of the field are *all* my friends back in Boo Hexico. I miss the forest creatures so much already. It's going to be difficult being away from them and my family for so many months."

Frankie couldn't imagine what it would be like to be away from home for so long! She felt even more determined to make sure Isi felt totally at home at Monster High. She smiled at her new ghoulfriend and placed a hand on her shoulder. "All of us at Monster High will feel like family to you soon enough—just wait and see!"

Isi smiled back, and Frankie hoped that she had made her feel at least a little bit better. "Do you have a big family in Boo Hexico?" she asked.

"Yes. And we are all very close."

"I would love to have a large family," Frankie said wistfully. "At least, I think I would. Clawdeen Wolf—she's one of my beast ghoulfriends and you'll meet her soon—has a huge family, and she's always telling me it's not always as great as it seems. But I think it would be amazing to have a pack like Clawdeen's. Always someone to hang out with, all that energy surrounding you day after day..."

Before Isi could say anything more, Cleo de Nile came around the corner. "Are you ready for your project presentation, Frankie?" Cleo asked with a friendly smile.

Frankie cringed. For just a few minutes, she had forgotten about her doomed project presentation and her missing pet. She checked the time and realized she and Isi had to hustle if they were going to make it to class on time. She didn't want Isi to be late on her first day! "As ready as I can be..." she said with a worried smile. Then she introduced Isi to Cleo.

Cleo stepped forward with a huge smile and said, "Well, hello there," as she brushed her shimmering hair off her shoulders. "I'm sure I need no introduction?" Cleo was the daughter of Egyptian royalty, the captain of the Fearleading squad, and one of the most popular ghouls at Monster High. It wasn't unusual for her to assume someone new to Monster High already knew who she was! But Isi didn't seem to mind. She smiled warmly at Cleo and introduced herself. A moment later, Cleo spotted her sweetie, Deuce Gorgon, and said, "Gotta go—but I'm sure I'll see you around!"

As they made their way toward class, Frankie told Isi all about the independent study projects that were due that day. "I'm really nervous about standing up there to give my presentation," Frankie admitted, leading Isi to a seat in the middle of the classroom.

"Presentations make me nervous too," Isi said sympathetically. "With bright lights shining right in my eyes, I tend to freeze up."

Frankie nodded. "Exactly. Also, things didn't turn out quite as well as I had hoped they would. I had this plan to bring in a special invention I made in my dad's lab, but—"

Before Frankie could tell Isi anything more about what had happened with Zappit, Mr. Rotter came into the room and asked everyone to be seated so class could begin. Frankie was sorry she couldn't tell Isi the rest of the story—she felt sure that Isi would understand how hard it had been for Frankie to lose her new creature, especially since Isi had told her about her close relationship with the animals that lived near her home in Boo Hexico.

"I'm sure you'll be fawntastic," Isi whispered, giving Frankie a reassuring smile.

But Frankie wasn't so sure. She had pictures of her time in the lab to share, but that was it—after all that hard work, she didn't have much to show for it. Would anyone believe that her project had been a success? Her dear, sweet Zappit was gone, and Frankie's project was incomplete. She'd hoped to demonstrate how her little pet could spin and dance around the table, and let everyone hear her adorable little roar. *Oh well*, Frankie thought. She took a deep breath and tried to calm herself.

"We have a lot of project presentations to look forward to today," Mr. Rotter said. "So we had best get started. I trust you all had a productive scaremester break, and that I will be impressed with the work you've done?" There was a murmur of agreement from all the students in class. The presentations began, and as student after student was called up to share their work, Frankie grew more and more nervous.

Then, near the end of class, she heard her name: "Frankie Stein? Are you ready to share your project with the class?"

Diary Entry

Well, that wasn't as bad as I'd thought it would be! It was so hard to stand up in front of everyone and talk about Zappit—it made me miss her even more! But people seemed really impressed with my project, and everyone asked really good questions about how things work in Dad's lab.

I feel like my classmates learned a lot about my family during my presentation. And I learned a lot about myself while I was finishing it! Who would ever have guessed I was <u>built</u> to work in the lab?!

I am really <u>proud</u> of the work I've done. And it feels voltageous to know that Dad is proud too.

Now I just wish I knew Zappit was okay.... Until I know she's safe at home again, I'm going to be monstrously worried.

Frankie

CHAPTER SIX

F rankie, I have something important to tell you!" Isi danced up to Frankie after class and pulled her aside.

"What's wrong?" Frankie asked.

"Last night, when I took an evening walk in the forest, I came across a beautiful clearing. As I was dancing in the glow of the moonlight, a small creature emerged from the darkness to join me. The two of us spent some time in the quiet of the forest together, then went our separate ways.

I realized during your presentation that the creature I danced with was your creation—Zappit!"

Frankie stared at her new ghoulfriend. "You have Zappit?"

Isi shook her head. "I was with her for a short while last night, but I don't know where she is now. Sometimes when I dance, it's like I'm in another world. When I finished my evening dance, she simply wandered off. She was there beside me one moment and gone the next. I thought nothing of it, because creatures often join me in the forest back home, then go off on their own adventure again."

"Do you know if she's okay?" Frankie asked, her stomach fluttering with nerves.

"I feel certain that she is," Isi said confidently. She put her hands on Frankie's arms and said, "She was alone when I met her, but she seemed to be at peace. If she had needed something, I believe she would have asked for my help. I have a way with animals—they are often drawn to me. And now that I know she has a family who is searching for her, I think I'll be able to help you find her again and bring her home."

"Oh, could you?" Frankie exclaimed. She was so lucky to have the perfect new ghoulfriend who could help her find Zappit—someone who had seen her! Isi could show them where she'd seen her, and that would narrow their search.

"Of course I will help you," Isi promised. "We can go out together right after school. Working together, we're sure to find her."

Frankie wrapped her arm through Isi's. "Thank you so much, Isi."

Isi laughed as she danced down the hall beside Frankie. "Don't thank me yet. We haven't brought her home—but we will. And, Frankie, you need to remember that animals are very resourceful—even creatures that were created in a lab." She smiled reassuringly. "I'm sure she'll be able to take good care of herself until she's home again. And we *will* get her home. I know it."

Frankie released a big sigh. "Having you around right now is making me feel so much better. I'm so glad you came to Monster High when you did! I don't know what I'd do without you." She squeezed Isi in a hug. "You made my whole day freaky-fabulous, you know!"

The rest of the morning flew by. At lunch, Frankie introduced Isi to the rest of her ghoulfriends—she was so excited they would get to add a new ghoul to their group of friends! The two other Monster Exchange ghouls joined them too. Kjersti and Ghoulia seemed to be in their own little world, comparing high scores in their favorite video game. Even though they hardly said a word to each other as they played on their handhelds, their random glances at each other's screens and periodic laughter made it clear they were bonding already.

Batsy and Venus had obviously hit it off right away too. They were talking about starting up a new club at Monster High to bring aware-ness to endangered plants and species. Frankie smiled happily at the ghouls around her table. It felt like everything was working out just as it should.

Partway through lunch, though, Isi sud-denly leaped up. "There's Twyla!" she exclaimed. "Frankie, thank you so much for inviting me to join you and your ghoulfriends for lunch, but if you don't mind, I'm going to run over and catch up with Twyla. I was looking for her all morning, and there she is, finally!" She smiled happily at Frankie, then gathered up her things and pranced over to Twyla's table in the cafeteria.

Frankie watched her go. *Isi had been looking*

for Twyla all day? Did that mean she didn't enjoy the time she spent with me? Frankie wondered. She suddenly felt a little hurt and wasn't entirely sure why.

"Don't look so down, Frankie," Lagoona Blue said, glancing over at Twyla's table. Twyla was greeting Isi, and the two were hugging. "Didn't you say Isi and Twyla already know each other? It makes perfect sense that they would sit together at lunch, don't you think? It's great that she's already made such a close ghoulfriend here at Monster High."

"You're right," Frankie said, trying to shake off her hurt feelings. She couldn't explain it, but she felt a little bit sad that Isi didn't want to sit at their table after spending the whole morning together. Frankie told herself that just because she was Isi's Monster Exchange buddy, it didn't mean they had to spend *all* their time together.

Even beast fiends spent time apart sometimes! She smiled at Lagoona. "Of course she would want to get caught up with Twyla. I know they haven't seen each other for a while."

Frankie and her ghoulfriends spent the rest of their lunch period catching up on what everyone had done during the scaremester break. Clawdeen entertained them all with stories of the extended family who had come to visit—she'd been stuck babysitting, and her stories about the mischief her twin cousins got into were a total scream!

But after lunch, the afternoon dragged. Frankie couldn't wait for the end of the school day to come so they could start the search for Zappit again.

She met up with Isi at her locker after school and waited while her buddy packed up her things. Then the two ghouls hustled across the school grounds to meet up with Lagoona, Clawdeen, Draculaura, and Cleo. Cleo had even offered to cancel Fearleading practice that afternoon so the whole squad could help with the search.

When Batsy and Venus found out there was a group heading into the forest near Monster High to look for a missing creature, they both offered to come along and help too. Batsy was eager to explore the natural habitats around Monster High, and both ghouls seemed sure they could help Frankie spot prints or other signs of Zappit's movements.

Isi had also told Twyla about Frankie's missing pet, and Twyla had offered to join the search party. Frankie was grateful. The more monsters who were out looking for Zappit, the better! And Frankie noticed that Isi seemed extra joyful when Twyla was around. They really did make a voltageous pair.

Back inside Monster High, Ghoulia and Kjersti were working together to figure out if there was some way they could find Zappit using a computer-based tracking device. Frankie had a feeling that even if they didn't figure something out before Zappit was found, neither ghoul would give up until they had designed a program that could help their fellow students if they ran into this sort of problem in the future.

"Thank you so much for helping, ghouls," Frankie said to the creepy-cool search crew that had gathered. "I'm not sure what the best way to do this is, but I was thinking maybe we could split up into groups of two or three so we can search more places?" She looked to her ghoulfriends for ideas.

"It might actually be a good idea to start our search as a group—stick together as a pack?" Isi suggested. "Every one of us has unique talents. If we use our strengths together and focus our search in the area where I saw her last night, we might have a better chance of finding Zappit more quickly."

"That's a good idea, Isi," Frankie agreed, once again grateful to have her new ghoulfriend there helping. "Why don't you lead the way, since you're the one who saw her last?"

The group set off quickly, away from the gates of Monster High. Isi danced along in the lead, guiding them all through a park and into the woods near school. "This is where I went walking last night," she said. "The clearing where I was dancing when I encountered Zappit is up ahead. Just through the woods a short ways."

"These shoes don't do woods. Isi might be comfortable hoofing it through sticks and leaves, but I definitely am not," Cleo muttered. Then she glanced at Frankie, who looked so worried about her missing creature, and released a deep sigh. She blew a kiss to her shoes. "Farewell, my golden lovelies. Into the woods we go. For Frankie."

As they made their way through the trees, the pack of ghoulfriends fanned out and shouted, "Zappit! Zappit, where are you?"

At one point, Frankie thought she saw something moving in a tree high above her. She unstitched her arm and sent it scuttling up the tree for a closer look. But it came back empty-handed, so Frankie realized she was probably just imagining things.

Clawdeen raced after something small that darted into a thick grove of trees, but she too found nothing. Venus and Batsy rooted carefully under low-hanging branches and plants, but the only things they found were a few interesting animal tracks and a small, empty den that some creature had recently used for a bed.

Before long, the group emerged on the other side of the woods. Cleo dusted herself off. Beside her, Clawdeen picked a few thorns out of her thick hair. "I'm so sorry, Frankie," Isi said sadly. "I really thought we might find her here. But don't worry...we won't give up hope— every one of us will continue to search until we find her."

Diary Entry

I'm so grateful that Isi and the other Monster Exchange ghouls have been willing to help me look for Zappit—I truly have the most voltageous ghoulfriends—new and old! And it was creeperific of Cleo to cancel Fearleading practice today (and even sacrifice a killer pair of shoes!) so all the ghouls could help. I am so lucky!

But I'm still so worried about my little pet! Isi keeps telling me that she believes Zappit is fine, and I trust her instincts. She's lived around animals all her life, so she knows a lot about them.

This morning, Dad told me Zappit's charge should last for at least a few more days before she powers down. I really hope we find her before she runs out of juice. Ugh. I'm hoping for some breakthrough that might get us closer to solving the mystery of where she's gone. Fingers crossed...but in the meantime, I have an idea that will let me feel like I'm doing something, even if I can't be out searching all night long!

Frankie

CHAPTER
SEVEN

As the afternoon light faded away, the ghouls agreed to split up and continue their search. Dinnertime came and went, but still Frankie wasn't ready to give up the hunt. She, Draculaura, and Clawdeen continued to search in their little group until the last light of day was extinguished. By the time night rolled around, even Frankie had to admit that they needed to take a break until morning.

After saying good night to her ghoulfriends,

she ran home to greet Watzit. Frankie had missed him so much while she was away at school—somehow the search for Zappit had made her even more eager to spend extra time cuddling Watzit when she got home.

"Hey, Dad?" Frankie said, poking her head into the lab after she and Watzit had played a quick game of fetch. He trailed behind her, then settled into his little bed in the lab for a snooze. Frankie could tell Watzit had begun to enjoy his time in the lab almost as much as she did.

"Frankie!" her dad exclaimed, looking up from his lab bench. "Did you find Zappit yet?"

Frankie shook her head sadly. "Not yet. We've been searching for hours, but there are just so many places she could be hiding."

Mr. Stein pulled her close for a hug. "You'll find her. And you needn't worry about her safety—I'm sure she's going to be just fine."

"That's exactly what Isi said," Frankie said, nodding. "It's hard not to worry, though. She's my first creation! I just can't believe she's gone."

Mr. Stein smiled. "I understand exactly how protective an inventor can feel about his creations," he said, smiling at her. Then he looked at his watch and gasped. "Speaking of my creations, I can't believe *you* are still awake! Look at how late it is, Frankie!"

"I couldn't get to sleep when I knew you were still in here working," she admitted.

"Ah," her dad said, grinning. "Do you have the inventor's curse?"

"What's that?" Frankie asked.

"Does the lab call to you, even when you should be doing other things?" he said.

"I guess a little bit," she admitted.

Mr. Stein rubbed his hands together. "Excellent! And are you so distracted by your ideas that it's sometimes hard to stop working for meals or friends or other activities?"

"I'm not as bad as you yet, Dad," Frankie said with a laugh. "I always have time for meals and my ghoulfriends! Mom is right, you know...you probably should get out of the lab a little more often."

Mr. Stein shrugged. "Yeah, I guess I really should."

"Also," Frankie said, "I had an idea. Want to talk about it over a snack upstairs?"

Mr. Stein looked around the lab sadly. "You want me to go upstairs and leave my precious—" He broke off suddenly and looked at her sheepishly. "What I meant to say is, of course I would love to go upstairs and enjoy a snack and a chat with my precious daughter."

As they made their way up the stairs, Frankie said, "I think it's a good thing I'm going to be spending more time working in there with you from now on, Dad. I'm going to make it my mission to help you remember that life exists outside the lab!"

"I like the sound of that!" Mrs. Stein said, greeting her husband and daughter inside the kitchen. "Sounds like you have some very good advice for your dad, Frankie."

Mr. Stein laughed as he made himself a cup of tea. "So what's this idea you've had?"

Frankie grabbed a cookie from the cookie jar and took a big bite. "I was wondering if you've ever had any luck creating a tracking device in the lab. I was sort of inspired by this GPS tracking program Ghoulia and one of the new Monster Exchange ghouls started working on today. It got me thinking... maybe we could try to build something in the lab that would help me find Zappit? Something with magnetism or something?"

"Hmm," Mr. Stein said. "Interesting. Perhaps magnetism and…" He began muttering to himself, and Frankie and her mom exchanged a look.

"So?" Frankie asked, nudging him to get his attention back. "Think it's possible?"

"Sure, it's definitely possible. I'm not sure it's something we could put together overnight, but I can certainly try." He pulled his eyebrows together in concentration, and Frankie could tell his mind was already whipping through possible designs and specifications in his head. "I like the way you're thinking!"

"Can we start to work on it right away?" Frankie begged.

Mr. and Mrs. Stein exchanged a worried look. "It's very late," said Mrs. Stein. Then she added, "But if working in the lab will help you feel like you're doing something more to find your pet, then I suppose you could spend a little while in there with your dad tonight."

"As long as your homework is done," Mr. Stein added.

"All done with my homework already!" Frankie cheered. Cramming her fall project into just a few days had taught her not to wait until the last minute again! She shoved the last of her cookie in her mouth, then dashed toward the stairs. "Let's get started right away."

By the time Frankie and her dad closed up the lab for the night, they had already made great progress on a search bot. Mr. Stein promised Frankie he would continue to work on it the next day while she was at school. He hoped to have it ready by the time school was out.

Frankie was exhausted when she finally went to bed—working in the lab was both exhilarating and exhausting. She curled around Watzit and then fell into a deep, dreamless slumber. When she woke in the morning, she checked Zappit's charging station in the lab, just in case her little creature had returned in the night. But as she knew would be the case, there was still no sign of her. Frankie got dressed quickly and rushed to school, posting more MISSING signs everywhere between her house and Monster High.

As Frankie unloaded her things in her locker, Isi rushed up and squealed, "I found Zappit!"

Frankie threw her arms around Isi. "That's voltageous! So where was she?"

Isi took a deep breath. "Right where I saw her the first night. Last night I went back there. When I closed my eyes and danced in the light of the moon, I felt something creep up beside me. I opened my eyes, and there she was! It was almost as though she had been waiting for me to come to dance."

"Seriously?" Frankie asked. "Do you think she was hiding out in the forest that whole time? I thought I saw something moving in one of the trees yesterday—do you think it could have been her? I bet the tracks Batsy and Venus found were hers!"

"Possibly," Isi said, nodding. "It's also possible she was hiding from us. She seems very shy, and she resisted following me when I called to her."

"So where is she now?" Frankie asked, hustling along beside Isi as they made their way to their first class.

Isi took a deep breath and looked Frankie in the eyes. Frankie could sense something was wrong. Isi told her, "When she came to my side last night, I checked her over right away to make sure she wasn't hurt. Then I tried to lead her out of the woods, but as soon as we neared the edge of the forest, she stopped and wouldn't move any farther." Isi's eyes filled with tears, and she said, "I'm so sorry, Frankie. I helped her build a small, cozy den on the edge of the woods. I checked on her as soon as I woke this morning, and she was content and as happy as can be." Isi smiled. "She's just the sweetest little creature—I must admit, spending time with her was such a comfort to me last night. I went into the forest feeling sad about missing my family. And then Zappit was at my side, and I instantly felt so much better. Being near her somehow made me feel less homesick."

"Oh, Isi," Frankie said, nearly bursting at her seams with relief. "I am so sorry to hear you were feeling so homesick! I'm glad Zappit brought you some comfort! Thank you for taking care of her last night. Will you show me where her den is after school? I can come pick her up there!"

Isi paused, and Frankie thought she saw a brief flicker of sadness pass across her ghoulfriend's face. "Why don't I bring her to you?" Isi said finally. "Now that she has danced with me, I believe we have bonded, and I think she has grown to trust me. Maybe if she and I dance to your house together, she might feel more comfortable being led out of the woods. She seems to have decided she loves my dancing," Isi said with a shrug and a smile. "Besides, if I bring her to you, I can see where she was created. Your dad's lab sounds so freaky-fab!"

"That would be great! And you're right—Dad's lab is totally voltageous," Frankie grinned. "I can introduce you to Watzit too."

"Who's Watzit?" Isi asked.

"Watzit was my first pet. My dad created him for me out of spare parts he had in the lab. He's part of the reason I created Zappit in the first place! I'm hoping the two of them will like having each other to hang out with during the day while I'm away at school."

"What a nice idea," Isi said. "Watzit is a very lucky pet."

Frankie settled into her seat next to Draculaura, making sure there was an open seat for Isi on her other side. Then she told Isi, "Watzit loved having me around last week during the scaremester break. I bet he's sad that Zappit ran off before they ever really got a chance to get to know each other. I can't wait to see the two of them playing together.... It will be so cute!"

Suddenly, Isi frowned.

"What is it?" Frankie asked.

Isi shook her head. "It's just...some animals are solitary creatures, Frankie. There are many animals who prefer to spend their time alone."

"How sad!" Frankie exclaimed. "All alone?"

Isi laughed. "Many animals love to be alone— some monsters too. Not everyone longs for a pack, like you do. Some creatures take comfort when they're in smaller groups or solo. Like Twyla—she prefers the company of just a few ghoul-friends, rather than many."

"Do you think that's why Zappit ran away?" Frankie asked worriedly. "Because she wanted to be alone?"

"It's a possibility," Isi admitted. "She seemed so shy when she approached me in the forest, and she waited until it was quiet to join me. This is just something to consider. It's possible she didn't know what to do when faced with the company of a little creature like Watzit."

Frankie was shocked. She hadn't even considered the possibility that her two pets wouldn't get along! She had assumed that they would hit it off as instant BMFFs. After all, they were designed in the same lab—they were destined to be buddies, weren't they?

"I may be monstrously wrong," Isi said when she noticed the concerned look on Frankie's face.

"But it is one possible explanation." Suddenly, she spotted Twyla across the room and waved. "Oh, Frankie—I told Twyla I'd sit with her during class today. Want to join us?"

Frankie glanced over at Draculaura. "I'm going to stay here with Draculaura. We always sit next to each other...."

"Okay, then if you don't mind, I'm going to go over there!" Isi said as she gathered up her books.

Frankie felt a pang of jealousy. Didn't Isi want to spend as much time together as she did? She shook it off and said, "Of course I don't mind. I'm so glad you and Twyla are becoming such good ghoulfriends."

Isi grinned and walked across the classroom to take a seat in the back, next to Twyla.

"Isi seems so sweet," Draculaura said, leaning in close to Frankie just as class was starting. "She and Twyla make a great pair."

"They really do," Frankie agreed. Twyla and Isi were a perfect match—just like she, Draculaura, and Clawdeen made a voltageous threesome.

"Have you told her about the Fearleading squad?" Cleo asked, turning around in her seat. "I've seen her dancing around in the halls, and it seems like she could be a fab fearleader! I'd love to have her on our squad!"

"I haven't talked to her about activities yet," Frankie said. She felt a twinge of regret that she'd been so focused on the search for Zappit, she'd forgotten to do everything she could to make Isi feel at home as part of the Monster High community. Was that why Isi didn't want to spend more time with her? "But I will! Promise."

All through class, Frankie thought about how glad she was to have Isi as a new ghoulfriend—thanks to her she would probably get Zappit back that very afternoon! And, on top of that, Frankie already had an idea for her next lab creation thanks to Isi. She couldn't wait to get started on it just as soon as Zappit was home again.

Diary Entry

I was <u>so excited</u> to see Zappit when Isi brought her home to me today that I sparked like crazy! I almost zapped poor Zappit! Zappit was being shy around me, but I think she was happy to be home. At least I hope so!

It was so much fun showing Isi around Dad's lab today! He showed her all his creeperific machines and even let her combine two beakers of liquid to let her see what would happen. She <u>totally</u> freaked out when the new mixture started fizzing and spitting. She dropped it, and the whole thing exploded in sparks. Dad and I both cracked up, but Isi didn't think it was quite as funny. She grabbed Zappit for comfort, then she and my little creature rubbed noses and danced around together. The two of them really do have a connection. I'll have to be sure to invite Isi over to visit her a lot.

My dad was acting super proud when he starting telling Isi all about how I'd constructed Zappit with almost no help from him—and also about my idea for the tracking bot. I love this special bond I have with him. I can't wait to tell him my plan for what I'm going to build next.

After Dad gave Isi the lab tour, she and I hung out in my room for a while, watching Zappit and Watzit while they played. Or, more like, not played. My two pets don't really have the connection I thought they would...but I'm hoping if I give them some time, they'll get their gears in sync. When we first got to my room, Watzit wouldn't stop barking, so Zappit started growling. Then, after a few minutes of sniffing each other curiously, they retreated to opposite ends of the room and curled up—Watzit at my side, and Zappit beside Isi.

So scary-cute! Well, I guess we'll see how things go. I'll get Zappit charged up, then the two of them can take all day tomorrow to get to know each other better.

Frankie

After Isi left that night, Frankie joined her dad in the lab again. "I have an idea for what my next invention should be," she announced. Watzit was already curled up in his bed on the floor of the lab, while Zappit charged nearby.

Mr. Stein looked up, obviously pleased. "You're really cranking out ideas, sweetheart. What are you going to make this time?"

Frankie smiled. "So, the thing I've learned since meeting Isi is that she's really missing her family. She's very close to them, and when she's home, she told me she spends a lot of time in the woods with the animals who live nearby. Today, I was thinking it might be fun to build a pet for her too. She and Zappit hit it off right away, and I think it would help make it easier for her to be away from her family if she had a little critter she could care for."

Mr. Stein nodded. "That sounds like an excellent plan. Do you need my help?"

"Nope," Frankie said happily. "You're such a great teacher that I think I've actually got the hang of it this time! Practice makes perfect, right?"

"That's absolutely right," he said. He put one hand on her shoulder and added, "You're proving what a great friend you are, Frankie. It seems as though you've gone out of your way to be kind and welcoming to Isi, and she's lucky to have you around this week."

"I'm so glad I've had her around too," Frankie agreed. "I don't know if I ever would have found Zappit without her help."

"That's true," Mr. Stein agreed. "You're lucky to have each other. It really proves what a special ghoul you are that you would be willing to give up one of your own lab creations to comfort a friend. I'm proud of you."

Frankie buzzed with happiness. "Thanks, Dad."

Mrs. Stein poked her head around the corner to see what was cooking in the lab. "How are you two crazy inventors doing down here?" she asked.

"We're voltageous!" Frankie answered. She invited her mom over, and told her about her plans to create Isi a pet of her very own.

"You sure do seem to be hitting it off," Mrs. Stein noted. "Is Isi getting along well with your other ghoulfriends too?"

"Yeah. Everyone really likes her. I think she's going to be such a great addition to our group," Frankie said. Then she frowned slightly. "The only thing is..."

After a pause, her mom prompted, "The only thing is...?"

"Well, it's just that Isi seems to be more interested in Twyla than she is in me and my ghoulfriends. She's really nice to us and everything and we get along great, but it just seems like she's really connecting with Twyla. I think maybe she prefers Twyla over us."

"Is that a bad thing?" Mrs. Stein asked gently. "Isn't it good that she's becoming close with another ghoul at school so quickly?"

"Well, yeah, I guess." Frankie chewed her lip.

"You don't sound so sure," Mr. Stein said. "Is Twyla nice, or are you worried Isi is spending time with someone who isn't going to be a true ghoulfriend?"

Frankie gasped. "Oh no! It's not that at all. Twyla is voltageously nice! And she and Isi seem to have really bonded." As she talked to her parents, Frankie began to realize something. "It's just, I sort of thought Isi and I would be *beast* ghoulfriends. I mean, I am her buddy in the exchange program and all, so I thought we would really hit it off. Isn't that the way it's supposed to work? Ghoulia and Kjersti act like they were programmed for each other, and Venus and Batsy are like two petals on the same flower. I just assumed Isi and I were meant to have perfect chemistry too...."

Mrs. Stein tilted her head as she thought about what Frankie had said. "I don't think that's the point of the buddy program, Frankie. You're supposed to be her guide—to help her find her way during her first week. You're not necessarily supposed to become beast ghoulfriends. That sort of special connection doesn't always happen, and it certainly can't be forced."

"I know!" Frankie said, feeling frustrated. Everything her mom said made sense, but Frankie still felt bad. "I just thought…" She didn't know how to explain what she thought. That she and Isi would become fast ghoulfriends, and then—what? Frankie already had so many creeperific ghoulfriends including Draculaura, Clawdeen, and everyone on the Fearleading squad. Of course, they always had room for more in their group, but did that mean Isi had to pick them as her main pack?

Mrs. Stein smiled and put her arm around her daughter. "Frankie, I love that you're so excited to get to know and love every ghoul at Monster High, but you can't be beast ghoulfriends with *everyone*."

Frankie nodded. Her mom was right, of course. She knew she shouldn't feel jealous about Twyla and Isi spending so much time together. Just because she and Isi weren't becoming beast ghoulfriends didn't mean they couldn't be ghoul-friends at *all.* "You're totally right, Mom. And you too, Dad." Her parents smiled. "I just want everyone to have a ghoulfriend—and I should be happy that Isi has already really hit it off with Twyla! Right?" She grinned.

"Right," her parents agreed.

Her mom added, "You know you can always talk to us about this stuff, right, Frankie?" Frankie nodded. Then her mom gave her a quick kiss on the cheek and said, "Twenty minutes until bed. Deal?"

Frankie leaned over to give her mom a hug. "Deal." She felt so much better after talking things out with her parents. She had just been so worried about helping Isi fit in and finding Zappit and keeping Watzit happy the last few days—it was easy to get carried away with all the things buzzing around in her head!

Mr. Stein returned to his own work then, while Frankie got started drawing up the plans for her newest creation. She tried to think about what kind of pet Isi would love most. Since Isi loved the outdoors, Frankie knew she should develop a pet that would enjoy taking walks with her in the woods. She scribbled some notes and began to sketch a few ideas. But she was having a hard time coming up with the perfect pet for Isi. For some reason, her mind kept wandering back to Zappit.

Frankie hadn't made a lot of progress before her mom poked her head around the corner of the lab again and cleared her throat. "Tonight you *both* need to get some rest. Last night, you were up until all hours working down here—tonight, I'm forcing you *both* to take a break from the lab!"

Frankie and her dad looked at each other and laughed. Mr. Stein put his hands up in surrender and said, "Fine, fine. She's right, you know—all of this will be waiting for us here tomorrow. I suppose it is important to take a break from your work every once in a while to let your mind recharge."

"I couldn't have said it better myself," agreed Mrs. Stein.

Diary Entry

When I woke up this morning, I knew right away that something was wrong. Watzit was snuggled up next to me, but when I reached down to pet Zappit, I realized my new little creature was gone. Again.

I jumped out of bed and searched all over my room, then ran into the lab to check the charging station. She was nowhere to be found. Obviously, my little escape artist had managed to get out for the second time.

Of course I'm upset that she's gone again, but this time I'm a little less worried. I know she'll be okay. And I'm also beginning to wonder if maybe Isi was onto something when she told me she thought Zappit preferred to be outside. Maybe she was also right about Zappit not really wanting to be around another creature all the time.

What if I'm trying to force Zappit and Watzit to get along and be beast friends, when really they're <u>not</u> meant to be BFFs? Maybe Zappit is actually better suited to someone else or somewhere else...?

Frankie

CHAPTER NINE

When Frankie got to school and ran over to tell Isi about Zappit escaping again, Isi laughed and said, "I know."

"What do you mean, you know?" Frankie asked.

"When I got up this morning to greet the sunrise and stretch my legs, I found Zappit curled up in the little den I helped her build on the edge of the forest. It seems she's comfortable there."

"I think you're right," Frankie said, nodding her head. "About that..."

Isi quickly said, "I'm really sorry, Frankie. I didn't realize she would fall in love with that den, or I wouldn't have helped her build it. It's just that when she came to me the other night and wouldn't follow me out of the forest, I wanted to do whatever I could to make her feel comfortable and at home until I could return her to you. Only now I think she might think that den *is* her home."

Frankie nodded again. "I'm so glad you did what you did when you found her alone in the woods! And, Isi, I'm beginning to wonder something...." Frankie paused. She thought back to the conversation she'd had with her parents last night—about how Isi and Twyla were a perfect match for each other, even though Frankie had been assigned as Isi's buddy—and how she'd been working on building a pet for Isi to make her feel more comfortable during the time she was at Monster High. Then she thought about her connection with Watzit, and the way Isi and Zappit seemed to have a similar connection. Suddenly, she knew exactly what she had to do to be a good friend. "I was wondering if maybe you want to care for Zappit," Frankie asked Isi. "For a while... or forever?"

"Are you serious?" Isi asked, her eyes wide. "I would love to take care of her! But I know how much you love her, and I don't know if I could take her away from you!" From the way her eyes shone, Frankie could tell she *wanted* to accept. Then Isi shook her head. "No, I couldn't take her from you. Zappit is your new pet! You created her. I'm sure there must be some way for us to help her learn that your house is her home."

In that moment, Frankie was absolutely certain that this was what she was supposed to do.

She didn't know animals as well as Isi did, but she could tell when someone needed a friend and some comfort. She could tell that Zappit was just the friend Isi needed...and Isi was the right person to help care for Zappit in the way she most needed to be cared for. "Please, will you take care of her?" Frankie asked, placing a hand on Isi's arm. "It's what I want. And I think she's just what you need. You are the perfect pair!"

Isi threw her arms around Frankie and cried, "Of course I will. Oh, thank you, Frankie!" She pulled away, and Frankie could see there were tears in her eyes. Zappit was just what Isi needed to make her feel perfectly at home during her Monster Exchange. Just like Frankie, Isi longed to be surrounded by family—and Zappit could be her family while she was away from home. "But please, will you let me do something for you too? To thank you for welcoming me to Monster High, and for sharing Zappit with me?"

"I don't need anything!" Frankie said with a smile. "Knowing you're happy here at Monster High is enough for me!"

"Please," Isi said. "I insist."

"What do you have in mind?"

"Come to the woods tonight," Isi said, beaming. "I want to show all of you what a harvest moon celebration is like! And you can give Zappit a hug. I'm sure she would love to show you her den."

Frankie buzzed through the rest of the day feeling more electrified than she had in days. She couldn't wait to go to Isi's party that night. Isi had invited everyone who wanted to come—including Watzit!—and they were all going to meet at moonrise in the clearing near the edge of the woods.

When school was out, Frankie rushed home to tell her parents about the party and to grab

Watzit. Watzit was just as excited as Frankie about the outing and trotted along happily by her side as they made their way toward the forest. When they arrived at the clearing in the forest, Frankie could see that a big bonfire was roaring. All her ghoulfriends were already fanging out, relaxing on rocks and tree stumps. It was a voltageous party!

As soon as she saw her approaching, Isi pulled Frankie into the circle. Frankie looked around at the group and saw the smiling faces of all her ghoulfriends—Clawdeen, Draculaura, Lagoona, Cleo, Ghoulia, Batsy, Venus, Kjersti, and, of course, Twyla. Zappit, who stuck close to Isi's side, poked her snout out and greeted Watzit timidly. The two sniffed each other curiously, then Zappit returned to Isi's side.

"Tonight," Isi announced to everyone, "we are having a harvest moon dance party in Frankie's honor!" Isi turned on some music. Spinning and dancing to the music, Isi took Frankie's hands in her own. "On the day we met," Isi said as they twirled through the firelight together, "you mentioned something to me about wishing you had a big family like me or a pack like Clawdeen. I've been thinking about what you said, and here's what I've realized: Even though you don't have any brothers and sisters, you *do* have a pack." She gestured around at the crowd of Frankie's ghoulfriends. "All of us. We're your pack. You bring us all together, like a family."

Frankie grinned happily. Isi was right, of course. Frankie had been wishing for a pack of her own, and here she'd had it all along.

Isi wrapped her arm around Frankie's shoulders and went on, "This week, the Monster High family—and you, especially—made me feel at home. Of course I miss my family back in Boo

Hexico, but with a family of friends surrounding me—and now Zappit!—I know I'll be just fine during my Monster Exchange. Thank you so much for being such a good ghoulfriend!"

Frankie pulled her in for a hug. "Oh, Isi, that's just so sweet of you to say. And you're right. These ghouls really are my pack! The best pack ever." She squeezed her new friend tighter. "And I'm so glad you're a part of it now."

"You know," Isi said, swaying beside her, "Zappit's still going to need a charge every once in a while."

"Oh!" Frankie gasped. "I almost forgot about that!"

"Here's what I was thinking…" She looked over at Zappit and Watzit, who were curled up happily on opposite sides of the fire. "Maybe she and I could come over once a week for a charge… and to fang out? I think I could get her to leave the woods every once in a while, as long as I promised to bring her back to her den to sleep!"

"I would love that," Frankie replied.

Zappit ran over then and nuzzled against Isi's leg. Frankie reached down to scratch her. Then she looked back at Isi and said, "The two of you are so well matched; it's almost as if she was made for you."

Isi smiled in the moonlight. "You're such a good friend, Frankie Stein, that I wonder if maybe somewhere deep down, you knew I was coming and would need a friend. So you created her—just for me."

Twyla suddenly approached the two ghouls from out of the shadows. She wasn't dancing with abandon like everyone else, but she was swaying a bit to the beat of the music. "Will you come join the group?" she asked, smiling shyly at Frankie and Isi. Frankie and Isi happily danced back over to where everyone else was. The whole gang spent the rest of the night talking and dancing and having a voltageous time under the harvest moon. With a pack like this, Frankie had a feeling this was going to be the best scaremester ever!

Diary Entry

Things with Isi have gone monstrously well during her first week at Monster High! She's already gotten to be great friends with a ton of ghouls at school, she and Zappit are getting along _perfectly_ together and enjoying their nightly moonlit walks through the forest, and some of the mansters at school are already falling head over hoofs for her. I have a feeling she's going to have a creeperific exchange scaremester at Monster High!

Oh, and the best thing of all: Isi is officially the newest member of the Fearleading squad!

Everyone got to see what a voltageous dancer she is at her harvest moon party. While we were dancing around the fire, Cleo asked Isi to come try out for the squad at this afternoon's practice. Before she got there, the ghouls and I were really struggling to learn the steps of a complicated new routine that needed a creeperific dance element, but we just couldn't get it right.

We didn't realize Isi had been watching us practice from just outside the door. All of a sudden, she stepped forward and offered to teach us the most amazing new dance. She's a natural teacher, and her dance was freaky-fabulous! Cleo was so impressed that she immediately invited her to join the squad! It turns out Isi's family is full of amazing dancers and she learned everything she knows from her ancestors. Isi has a feeling she was meant to come to Monster High so she could share a special part of herself with us!

I sure am glad she came to stay, or I might never have figured out what makes Zappit tick! Thanks to Isi, my first lab creation turned out to be a total success.

After this week as Monster Exchange buddies, I know Isi and I will be fawntastic friends forever. The funny thing is she thinks she owes me a special thanks for making her feel so at home at Monster High. And I think I owe her a <u>million</u> thank-yous for helping me find Zappit and care for her properly.

Really, neither of us owes the other anything. Because helping each other? <u>That's what ghoulfriends do!</u>

Frankie

Start your own voltageous diary, just like Frankie! On the following pages, write about your own creepy-cool thoughts, hopes, or screams...whatever you want! These pages are for your eyes only! (Unless you want to share what you write with your ghoulfriends!)

MONSTER HIGH

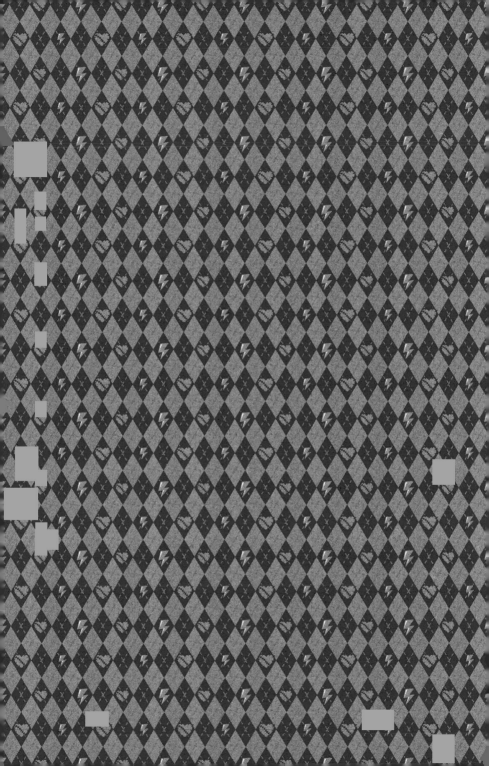

Did you 💙 reading Frankie's diary?
Then you will totes love reading

LAGOONA BLUE'S DIARY...
COMING SOON!